A HORSE NAMED
Funny Cide

A HORSE NAMED
Funny Cide

BY THE
FUNNY CIDE TEAM

ILLUSTRATED BY
BARRY MOSER

G. P. PUTNAM'S SONS

THE KENTUCKY DERBY is the biggest horse race in the world. Millions of people watch the Derby each year. The Derby is the first true test for a young thoroughbred—only three-year-old horses are allowed to run. And a horse who wins the Kentucky Derby can go on to greatness.

Because the Derby is so important, each horse's team will do all they can to help their horse's chance of winning. Sometimes they will spend more than a million dollars on their horse!

One year, a horse called Funny Cide ran in the big race. People didn't think he had much of a chance: His body was too narrow, his owners weren't rich, his trainer wasn't famous, and his jockey was too old. But like any race, once the Derby starts, any horse can win . . .

Baby Funny

When Funny Cide was born, not too many people noticed.

He was small for a newborn foal. His parents weren't famous racehorses, and he was born in New York—not Kentucky, where most of the great racehorses come from.

But he was perky and playful, and when the vet tried to give him his shots, he fought like crazy. That was a good sign—the little horse had a big heart!

As Funny got older, he grew bigger. But his body was still narrower than most racehorses. Even before he raced, it didn't look like he could be a champion.

But a man named Tony, who buys horses and prepares them to race, decided to take a chance. Tony's plan was to buy Funny Cide, work him into racing shape for eight months, and then sell him for more money. So Funny said good-bye to his home in New York, and headed down to Tony's barn in Florida.

At his farm, Tony left Funny alone to roam the fields and play in the stable with the other animals. Tony kept cats, ducks, and a goat named Cissy in the stalls. Sometimes it looked more like a zoo than a stable!

At first, Funny didn't like wearing a saddle or having a bit in his mouth to help a rider steer him. His riders had to talk to him like a schoolteacher: "Pick your feet up and pay attention, feet up, up, up. Quit messing around!"

But soon Funny found his rhythm. By now, he had filled out some and looked more like a thoroughbred. And when it was time to run, Tony didn't have to talk to him—Funny just decided to go.

Funny ran freely on a path, straight as an arrow. His coat was shining and he was running fast like a real racehorse. The time had come for Tony to sell him.

Barclay Tagg and his assistant, Robin Smullen, with Funny Cide

Tony called up a trainer named Barclay Tagg. Barclay was a good trainer and a good friend, but he had never had a great horse. Barclay took a look at Funny—he was a skinny red horse, but with brightness in his eyes, upright ears, and something thick and sturdy in his legs.

Barclay could tell that Funny had a lot of potential. So he talked to the men who would actually buy Funny Cide from Tony. Most of the time, a horse's owner is very, very rich, like a prince or a movie star. But Barclay worked for a group of old high-school friends just looking to have some fun owning a horse—and not spend too much money doing it!

Tony wanted $75,000 for Funny Cide. It wasn't the million dollars that a movie star might pay for a horse, but it still seemed like a lot of money to the group of friends. However, Barclay was sure Funny was worth it. Finally, the leader of the group, Jack, said to Barclay, "Okay, let's go get that horse. If you like him so much, then go buy him."

Tony was happy—he had made good money training Funny Cide—but he was sad to see Funny leave. He had grown to love the skinny red horse with fire in his belly. Like before, Funny Cide was loaded into a van and taken back home to New York.

When Funny Cide first got on the track at his new home at Belmont Park on Long Island, he galloped past every other horse. "He does everything so easy," Barclay told his assistant, Robin. But Funny was also hard to control. Soon enough, he injured his shins and couldn't race for the whole summer.

Funny spent four months getting back into shape on Long Island. He shared a barn with two cats, Freckles and Tuna, and they would often sleep together nose to nose. He also developed a taste for peppermints and doughnuts, and Barclay always kept a supply on hand to reward Funny for a good workout.

In August, at Saratoga Race Course, where he was spending six weeks, Barclay decided Funny was well enough to run again. He asked a jockey named Jose Santos to ride him in a morning workout.

As soon as Jose got on Funny, he felt Funny pull him away. Funny Cide was eager to race, and his gallop was awesome, a rolling, effortless feeling.

After half a mile, Jose slowed down and trotted back to Barclay. "What were you doing out there?" Barclay snapped. "You went forty-six and four."

Jose stared at Barclay. Had he really run the half mile in 46$^{4/5}$ seconds? That seemed impossible. "I didn't go that fast," he said.

"Yeah, you did. You went that fast."

Jose knew Funny was better than any horse he'd been on in a long time. Right away he called his agent. "Listen," he said. "Whatever you do, don't lose this horse. Keep me on this horse."

Jose and Funny Cide

Since Funny was training so well, Barclay told the owners it was time to run him in a race. He chose a race at Funny's home in Belmont Park and asked Jose to be the jockey. When the bell for the start of the race went off, Funny bumped into another horse and immediately fell behind. But soon enough, he picked up steam. At the finish line, he won by fourteen and three-quarters lengths—that's a landslide!

Since Funny ran so well, they decided to try Funny in a bigger race, the Bertram Bongard. Funny won that race, too. In fact, he broke the record for the race by a second!

But once fall came, Funny had a problem: He was having trouble breathing when he ran. He still won his next race, but Barclay was worried—the Kentucky Derby was next spring, and Funny wouldn't have a shot if he couldn't get all the air he needed to race as fast as he could.

So Barclay rested Funny for three months. But it didn't help. Funny lost his next race down in Florida, and everyone could tell he wasn't feeling well. They tried all kinds of treatment, but nothing seemed to help. It looked like the little horse had yet another obstacle in his way—and maybe one he couldn't beat.

Finally, a veterinarian figured out Funny's problem was in his throat. The best cure was simply to give him medicine just like a person with a cold. Barclay also strapped a gizmo called a transpirator over Funny's mouth—it worked like a humidifier so Funny could breathe steam and soothe his throat. The barn cats Freckles and Tuna must have thought Funny looked strange with the mask on his face!

The new treatment seemed to work, but Funny had lost a lot of training time. He did well in the next race, but he didn't win. Then, he went to the Wood Memorial, a very important race. And there, for the first time, he met Empire Maker.

Ever since he was born, people expected Empire Maker to win races. He was a huge horse, and his parents had both been big winners. He was from Kentucky, where great horses are supposed to be born, and he lived and trained at one of the best barns in the world.

Like everyone expected, Empire Maker won the race. But he didn't win by much. And guess who came in second? Funny Cide raced with the big horse stride for stride the whole way.

Everyone was ecstatic that Funny did so well. It meant something very important: Funny was ready to run in the Kentucky Derby.

Empire Maker and Funny Cide at the Wood Memorial

A lot of fancy people were not amused

For the little horse from New York, the Derby might have seemed overwhelming. Empire Maker would be there, along with all the other million-dollar superstars.

Funny's team could have been intimidated, too. People who own horses usually make a big show of going to the Kentucky Derby. They wear fancy clothes and hats, and they drive to the racetrack in fancy cars.

But Funny Cide wasn't fancy and neither were his owners. So no one paid much attention to Funny Cide. And that suited him just fine—right before the race was supposed to start, Funny lay down and took a nap!

Meanwhile, Jack and the rest of Funny's owners showed up at the track. They didn't come in a limousine—they arrived in a big yellow school bus. Nobody had seen anything like this before, and a lot of the fancy people weren't amused. But Jack and his friends were having fun—and that was the whole point, to have a good time.

When it was time for the big race, Barclay woke up Funny and led him out to the track. Suddenly Funny reared up and started kicking. Was he nervous? Barclay was worried, but as soon as Funny saw the other horses, he calmed down. It seemed like he recognized his opponents and knew what he had to do.

The horses lined up in the starting gate. *Clang*! the bell sounded, and they were off. Like in his very first race, Funny bumped another horse and briefly dropped back. But then he found an opening and surged forward. He had a clear path to the finish line. Would he be fast enough?

As Funny hurtled down the last stretch of the race, up in the stands Jack started chanting: "We're going to win the Kentucky Derby! We're going to win the Kentucky Derby."

And just like that, Funny Cide swept across the finish line. He had done it— the little horse with the big heart had won the 129th Kentucky Derby!

Funny Cide wins the Kentucky Derby

Afterward, no one could believe it. How did this narrow little horse—owned by a bunch of high-school buddies, conditioned by an old trainer who'd never won a race this big, ridden by a jockey who had never won the Derby—how did *this* horse win the biggest race of all?

Down in the winner's circle, the Funny Cide team all celebrated together. Because that was one reason why Funny had won the race—everyone had worked together to make him a winner. But there was another reason, too. As Barclay said, "He's really, really fast."

Once the Derby was over, it was time to get ready for the next important race, the Preakness. Funny's team loaded the horse onto a special airplane just for horses and flew him back home to Belmont Park.

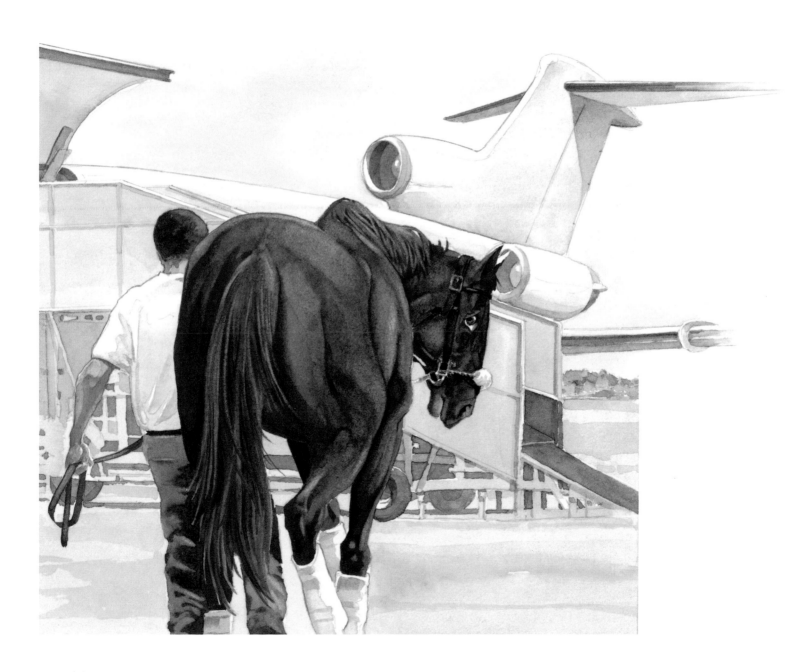

Things looked good for Funny: The Preakness was a shorter race, and Empire Maker wouldn't be running. But unlike the Derby, Funny was now the favorite to win, and everybody knew him. Mobs of people wanted to see his barn, and everyone in the press wanted his picture.

Throughout it all, Funny stayed relaxed. If anything, he seemed hungrier than usual—Barclay had to bring extra doughnuts to the barn!

The day of the race came, and once again, Funny Cide won. But this time, he was way ahead of the rest of the horses. In fact, it was the second-biggest margin of victory in the Preakness's history. This time, Jack and the other owners danced in a conga line down to the winner's circle. They even sang their old high-school fight song!

Winning the Preakness was very important. It meant that if Funny won the upcoming Belmont Stakes, he would win the Triple Crown. To win all three races in a row is the ultimate achievement in horse racing. No horse had won the Triple Crown in twenty-five years.

It seemed like everyone was rooting for Funny to win the Belmont. They liked the fact that his team was just a bunch of regular guys instead of princes and millionaires. Soon, Funny Cide T-shirts started showing up, then hats and buttons.

But while everyone was excited about Funny, Barclay was worried. Running three big races in five weeks was hard on any horse, let alone a small one like Funny Cide. When Funny trained, he seemed nervous and often would start to buck and kick.

To make matters worse, on the day of the Belmont Stakes it rained. This made the track muddy and difficult to run on. Plus, he had to race Empire Maker again, and Empire was healthy and well-rested from skipping the Preakness.

Once the race started, Jose could tell Funny was having trouble with the mud. He pushed ahead to the lead, but that wasn't necessarily a good thing—Funny might not have enough energy at the end to win. Sure enough, when the horses came around the last turn and headed for home, Funny didn't have anything left. Empire Maker won the race, and Funny crossed the wire in third place, beaten by five and a quarter lengths.

The Funny Cide team was heartbroken. But as Funny turned and walked back to his barn, something strange happened: The entire crowd in the stands started to cheer. At first, Jose thought it was for Empire Maker. But then he realized that the applause was for Funny Cide. The crowd seemed to be saying, "Thank you."

Funny Cide finishes third at Belmont

After the Belmont, everyone hoped Funny Cide would bounce back and win his next race. But things didn't get much better for the little horse.

At his next race, the Haskell Invitational, Funny came in third, and the next day he had a fever and a slightly injured eye. Just like with his throat problem, Funny took a long time to heal and didn't race again that summer.

Then, in the fall, he raced in the Breeder's Cup Classic, which is traditionally the last big race of the season. Not only was it far from home in California, but it was 101 degrees on the day of the race. Funny had never raced in weather that hot, and it showed: He came in ninth.

But in the end, none of that mattered. To people everywhere, Funny was still a great horse. That winter, all the sportswriters and horse people voted on the Eclipse Award for best three-year-old horse of the year. Once again, it came down to Funny Cide and Empire Maker. But like the Kentucky Derby, Funny Cide came out on top, beating the other horse 150 votes to 92.

When the Funny Cide team got together to celebrate, they all realized just how much Funny had enriched their lives. Both Barclay and Jose had seen their careers skyrocket in just a year. What had started out as a fun adventure for some high-school friends had turned into an unforgettable experience. Something about Funny had touched all of them deep inside. And his courageous journey down the track at the Kentucky Derby had inspired a world of fans.

And where was Funny himself? He was back at the barn with Freckles and Tuna, sucking on a peppermint—ready for the next race.

To all of Funny Cide's young fans—THE FUNNY CIDE TEAM

And for my friend Allie Crowe—BARRY MOSER

G. P. PUTNAM'S SONS

A division of Penguin Young Readers Group.

Published by The Penguin Group. Penguin Group (USA) Inc., 375 Hudson Street, New York, NY 10014, U.S.A.

Penguin Group (Canada), 90 Eglinton Avenue East, Suite 700, Toronto, Ontario, Canada M4P 2Y3 (a division of Pearson Penguin Canada Inc.). Penguin Books Ltd, 80 Strand, London WC2R 0RL, England. Penguin Ireland, 25 St. Stephen's Green, Dublin 2, Ireland (a division of Penguin Books Ltd.). Penguin Group (Australia), 250 Camberwell Road, Camberwell, Victoria 3124, Australia (a division of Pearson Australia Group Pty Ltd). Penguin Books India Pvt Ltd, 11 Community Centre, Panchsheel Park, New Delhi - 110 017, India. Penguin Group (NZ), Cnr Airborne and Rosedale Roads, Albany, Auckland 1310, New Zealand (a division of Pearson New Zealand Ltd). Penguin Books(South Africa) (Pty) Ltd, 24 Sturdee Avenue, Rosebank, Johannesburg 2196, South Africa. Penguin Books Ltd, Registered Offices: 80 Strand, London WC2R 0RL, England.

Library of Congress Cataloging-in-Publication Data

A horse named Funny Cide / by the Funny Cide Team ; illustrated by Barry Moser.   p.   cm.

1. Funny Cide (Race horse)—Juvenile literature. 2. Race horses—United States—Biography. I. Moser, Barry, ill. II. Funny Cide Team.

SF355.F86H67 2006   798.4'0092'9—dc22   2005020035   ISBN 0-399-24462-X

1 3 5 7 9 10 8 6 4 2

First Impression